PUKI HORPOCKET PRESENTS

BOO

THE GREATEST BOUNTY HUNTER
EVER TO SAIL THE BLACK

EARTH EDITION BY
ZACHRY WHEELER

eBook ISBN: 978-1-954153-18-9
Paperback ISBN: 978-1-954153-17-2
Edited by Jennifer Amon
Published by Mayhematic Press

PARENT SERIES

Puki Horpocket Presents is a spin-off series from *Max and the Multiverse*, in that it takes place on the massive Durangoni Space Station. The stories are intertwined, share many characters and settings, and can be read in any order you please.

EARTH EDITION

Greetings, Earthling!

My name is Zachry Wheeler and I'm a science fiction author based on Earth. I was chosen to serve as translator for all terrestrial editions of *Puki Horpocket Presents*, a literary series beloved throughout the universe.

It's been a great honor.

It's also been super stressful.

Decoding an alien tongue is daunting at a baseline, let alone through the prestigious lens of Puki Horpocket. He is renowned for his unique blend of commentary, interviews, and dramatic depictions. My job is to stick the landing for human readers. I sincerely hope that I do his words justice, but admittedly, I sometimes feel like a toddler translating Orwell.

The Durangoni Space Station is home to countless species and cultures, and thus, countless lexicons. Some things are universal, like beer. Other things are regional, like atmo barriers on artificial oceans. Some things are truly horrifying and do not warrant translation, regardless of their pop culture equivalents.

I did my best, but aliens be weird, y'all.

Puki Horpocket tales are chock-full of excitement, debauchery, and blatant disregard for delicate sensibilities. Fair warning: the language is lewd and the characters are crude, so keep your wits inside the vehicle and enjoy the ride.

CHAPTER 1

Few memberships are more coveted in the universe than the Bounty Hunters Union of Durangoni, and for good reason. The healthcare is top-notch, the vacation is generous, and its members are regarded as the very best in the business. They are the rockstar pirates of the great black sea, sailing under banners of pure adoration. Criminals will often pose for pictures when captured, elated by the prospect of their newfound prison cred.

The top five hunters in BHUD enjoy a cult-like celebrity status. There is Snigg the Snatcher, a brutish fellow known for his heavy-handed approach. Debaru Funk is a femme fatale. OBY-42 is a crafty android. Zybor is a straight-up murder hobo.

And then there's Boo.

Boo is the best of the bunch by a very wide margin. His stats are unmatched, unreachable, and damn near godlike. He is also one of the strangest creatures in the cosmos. While the other four command massive fan bases, Boo remains a peripheral oddity. It's a bizarre paradox, given his status as the top banana.

That is, until you meet him.

He wears basic clothes with basic colors, like a middle-aged dad with nothing left in the fucks tank. This does little to distract from a near-featureless head. "Near" being an important distinction, as his smooth white dome has a tiny slit for a mouth and nothing else. Despite the absence of eyes, ears, and nostrils, he tracks stimuli like anyone else, leading many to believe that he experiences the world in a wholly different spectrum. He also moves like a bedeviled phantom, which tightens every butthole when he enters a room.

I use "he" in reference to Boo based solely on his choice of dad-clothes. Truth be told, nobody knows *what* he is, or if "he" even applies. Boo is the sole member of his species living aboard the station, assuming that he's a species at all. Some think that he is an asexual mutant. Others suspect that he is a shapeshifting fungus. Many have asked Boo directly, but Boo's vocabulary is limited to a single word: "Boo." He rarely offers it, choosing to remain creepily silent like a goth kid at a frat party. When he does speak, it is soft and reflective, similar to the way most people use "Hmm."

Nevertheless, Boo remains the greatest bounty hunter ever to have lived. This is primarily due to a batshit bonkers strategy that is impossible to replicate, yet widely circulated as gossip and folklore. Everybody has a favorite Boo story, including the other bounty hunters. They often refer to the "Big Three," i.e. best hunts ever completed, all of which belong to Boo. This book will explore those remarkable tales and hopefully shine some light on one of the most eccentric artists in the universe.

But before we dive in, allow me to introduce myself. My name is Puki Horpocket. I am an editor at large for the Definitive Directory of Durangoni, the panoptic mega-wiki for the largest space station in the universe. Durangoni is home to a trillion active residents, all of whom access the directory for their daily wants and needs.

Want to try a new restaurant?

Consult the directory.

Need a doctor for your second spleen?

Consult the directory.

Want to see an acrobatic clown show?

Consult the directory.

Need the latest news on your favorite bounty hunter?

(drumroll) Consult the directory.

The Bounty Hunters Union of Durangoni enjoys extensive documentation within the directory, much of which I recorded myself. Each hunter has a detailed archive that is managed by a dedicated historian.

Save for one.

I have personally managed Boo's profile for the last several years. The first line reads, "Boo was born (presumption), stuff happened, then he arrived at Durangoni." It hasn't changed since the day it was entered, hence my fascination with his backstory. There is so much to learn about Boo and so much mystery that surrounds his existence. As a dedicated storyteller, I cannot help but be drawn to this delectable enigma.

But where to start?

After much consideration, I determined that the best course of action was to follow Boo's initial footsteps and start exactly where he did: at BHUD (pronounced Bee-Hud). I scheduled a meeting with the Union President, a legend in her own right by the name of Helga Naath. After brushing up on her personal history, I grabbed my proverbial pen and away I went.

* * *

Luckily for me, getting to the BHUD headquarters was a mere hop, skip, and jump to the nearest pod train station. As with most powerful guilds that called the station home, BHUD carried enough cachet to occupy a central ring. The Directory offices also qualified, for obvious reasons. The general rule of thumb was this: the bigger the clout, the wider the ring.

For anyone needing an explanation, the Durangoni megastructure formed a top-like shape, in reference to the boring children's toy. A massive set of disc-like rings rotated independently around a central axle. The largest ring in the center served as the main thoroughfare, featuring the majority of docking stations and high-end commerce. The poles were more specialized and required

3

some travel time to visit.

The pod train network fulfilled this need. It connected every ring through a complex web of service tunnels and express corridors. The pods themselves were magnetically linked with atmo barriers that allowed passengers to wander between them. They could break away as needed and race to the hidden bowels of the station. If your destination was highly peculiar, chances are that you arrived in a single pod.

My train was still a few dozen strong when it slowed to a stop at my destination. BHUD was located near the surface of a central ring, a ritzy locale filled with high fashion and low tolerance for dregs. To the average eye, it would seem like an odd place for a bounty hunter base, but we're not talking about dirty grifters with missing fingers (although some would qualify). The elite members of BHUD enjoyed the highest perks of celebrity stardom, second only to the core engineers that kept the station afloat. Thus, a typical client wasn't looking to collect a gambling debt. BHUD members were hired to change the social fabric of the universe.

The pod train doors slid open and I strolled into a gleaming corridor. A pleasant melody played in the background, highlighting a thin cloud of incense that wandered through the cool air. When the foot tunnels smelled like a spa, one could only imagine what the spas smelled like. Hologram signs with muted colorations directed visitors to their destinations. I followed my own towards the Cosmic Relations sector. It housed everything that involved delicate foreign matters, be them ambassador offices or murders for hire (often the same thing).

Given this sensitivity, CR offices were guarded around the clock. A separate passage with numerous checkpoints discouraged curious eyes from wandering too close. The stout frames of station security provided an effective visual deterrent. The CR sector was one of the few places where prestige counted for less than nothing.

No fans here, just the cold stares of justice.

My Directory ID card, on the other hand, opened every door. With a final flick and scan, the Cosmic Relations sector was revealed to me. Drab would be the overall vibe, as there was no one to impress with colorful advertisements. I could hear the words "gray is fine" from an architect in the distant past. Hologram signs floated above a series of alcoves, each denoting an occupant and current status. A quick scan uncovered BHUD, prompting a nod and continuation.

I opened the front door and entered a quiet lobby. At first glance, it presented as a branding salon, something for narcissists to charge other narcissists for lessons on narcissism. Life-sized decals of famous bounty hunters decorated the walls. Each of them was preened and posed, no doubt to capitalize on image rights.

There was one glaring omission, though.

Boo, it would seem, had no interest in such acclaim.

At the center of the room was a small desk with an intercom. No receptionist, just a single red button that read "Press for Help."

And so I did.

"Can I help you?" the intercom said.

"Yes. Puki Horpocket here to see Helga Naath."

"One moment."

Precisely one moment later, a door behind the desk slid open.

"Third door on the right," the speaker said.

"Thank you."

The intercom crackled away without response.

I proceeded around the desk and through the door, which promptly shut behind me. My gaze floated down a hallway with stark lighting and numerous doors, each with a hologram panel that denoted the current occupant. Most were vacant. It made sense, given the nature of the work. A hunter behind a desk isn't much of a hunter.

I located the door in question and gave it a firm yet unaggressive knock. Funny enough, this was a grave concern of mine. I knew how to assert myself to a variety of individuals. Directory intern? Vigorous knock, borderline hostile. Meek eyewitness? Gentle knock with a pleasant melody. But the president of an elite bounty hunter organization? After a rigorous analysis, I settled on "creepy uncle that needs a firm dressing down." In other words, knock like you mean it, but don't rattle the frame.

And so I did.

"Come in," said a muffled voice.

Nailed it, I thought, then opened the door.

My first impression was that of an interrogation room. Two chairs, one table, single light overhead, nothing on the walls but gray paint and fear. Helga sat on the opposite side with her feet up on the table. She swiped through a security tablet with the vigor of an annoyed teenager. A matte gray suit clung to her sturdy frame, one that could easily break me in half if so inclined. She embodied the grizzled veteran, someone who had paid her dues and now says "I'm too old for this shit" at parties.

With a final swipe, she tossed the tablet aside and met my gaze. Ebon eyes with white irises commanded my attention. Her silver hair was bound tight, tracing a sharp line around her dusky complexion. She radiated power and fortitude, enough to weaken my knees and hope for a quick death.

And thus began the inquiry.

What follows is my detailed exchange with Helga Naath, the highly respected president of a revered institution within the largest space station in the universe. In Durangoni terms, it was the closest I could get to interviewing royalty.

* * *

Hello, Ms. Naath. My name is—

So you're here to talk about Boo.

I—um, yes. How did you know?

You're Puki Horpocket, the guy known for telling outrageous stories about outrageous weirdos. If you're talking to me, then the mystery solves itself.

(I let out a nervous chuckle.) Guilty.

It's okay. You actually caught me at a good time.

(She motions for me to sit, which I do after a grateful smile and a polite bow of respect. I unzip my satchel, retrieve my notepad, and cross my legs for the coming exchange, all in a single well-practiced motion.)

So—

And what makes you think I'm going to tell you a goddamn thing?

(My jaw hangs open. The tension is sudden, sharp, and knots my stomach.)

(She laughs and slaps the table.) I'm just messing with you. We like to rib. Eases the stress.

(I laugh nervously.) Consider my stress eased, then. (It wasn't.)

So what would you like to know?

To start, I am curious to learn how Boo ended up in BHUD.

(shrugs) Showed up one day, nabbed a job, been crushing it ever since.

That's all you have?

Boo isn't the most forthcoming of blokes, so don't expect a dissertation. He's as mysterious in here as he is out there. That said, the stories are no less spectacular.

Fair enough. And given your experience with that mystique, I would be very curious to know what your favorite Boo story is.

(grunts and shakes head) Oh wow, so many to consider. The one that pops into mind is, of course, the single greatest feat in the history of bounty hunting.

The Hollow Hold Gambit.

Yes. But I also understand why *me* citing that would be uninteresting.

I still get into heated debates about the Galwock Terror, which I think is criminally underrated. But if I had to pick one, it would have to be the Jacothra Wander.

Isn't that one of the Big Three?

(nods) Generally a distant third to the first two. But when it comes to pure substance, the *virtue* of the hunt, it doesn't get any better than Jacothra.

And why is that?

I think it beautifully captures the essence of what makes Boo tick. He's a very odd bloke, but there's a method to his madness. It takes an extraordinary level of patience and discipline to catch the uncatchable, and that's exactly what he does, day in and day out.

That particular bounty was classified as UNO, or unobtainable, due to the target's resilience and lack of intel. UNO payouts are very high, but the opportunity costs make them unfeasible at best. Most are captured by accident, i.e. they just happened to show up during another hunt. Boo is the only hunter who takes UNOs as primary jobs.

This one only had two pieces of info. First, the target was Findellio Nomic, a highly skilled survivalist who worked as a scout for the Varokin Empire. That alone sent the bounty into the stratosphere. Highly desirable, if not for the second part.

Jacothra.

Exactly. Nomic was last seen on descent. Unobtainable, by definition.

And yet, Boo completed the job.

(nods) Amazes me to this day.

So why is it your favorite?

I understand the intrigue that surrounds the Gambit. It's an astounding achievement, a masterclass of awareness and coordination. But I would argue that the Jacothra Wander is equally astounding, albeit from the opposite end of the spectrum. If your goal is to paint a complete picture of Boo for your readers, then I would start there.

And who would best wield that brush?

You up for a drink? Buy a few rounds and I'll take you on that journey.

(I gasp and press both hands to my chest, pleading with my heart to resume normal function after skipping several beats. My voice lowers to a woozy whisper.)

Are you suggesting that we go to ... the *placc*?

(grins)

* * *

My panicked expression must have conveyed acceptance, because Helga rose from her chair and beckoned me to follow. If I were to describe my mental space at that exact moment, it would have been a swirling vortex of pants-shitting intrigue. After all, no one gets invited to the Golden Quiver (the cluster-famous pub for elite bounty hunters) without a damn good reason.

There were stories to tell, and Helga thought it best to hear them from the gloobur's third orifice (read: horse's mouth). First on the docket was the third-best bounty hunt of all time: the Jacothra Wander.

CHAPTER 2

When it comes to criminals and planets, there are places you go to hide and places you go to die. Jacothra was the latter. But for one wily fugitive, it was the perfect mix of both.

Findellio "Finny" Nomic made a name for himself as a Varokin scout. This was mostly due to his unique ability to weather the harshest climates. Finny was a subspecies of tardigrade that evolved a massive girth (read: water bears the size of actual bears). His skin was thick, his claws were sharp, and his cells were death-resistant. He could withstand a boiling storm of sulfuric acid with the same indifference of taking a lukewarm shower. This made him terribly useful to nefarious spy networks, which landed him a lucrative job with the Varokin Empire.

But alas, his amazing talents would lead to an equally amazing downfall.

Lord Essien, feared leader of the Varokins, decided that Finny's insider knowledge was too much of a liability. She tried to kill him, but failed, because tardigrade. He fled to a rival faction, but landed in the net of an undercover operation. Finny was arrested, imprisoned, and transferred to Durangoni for further processing.

But Durangoni, having no idea how shockingly immune Finny

was to punishment, would soon have egg on its face. Prisons were often used to source labor for hazardous projects, some of which produced toxic waste. Finny volunteered, then hid in a disposal tank. It was transported off-station for processing, which raised zero suspicion. No one had thought to dig through toxic sludge for stowaways, so he simply walked away from the dump site.

So where does a hyper-resilient fugitive go?

Of the top hellholes that come to mind, most would say Jacothra.

The air was poisonous, the soil was sulfuric, the water was acidic, and the critters that lived there were highly venomous. In fact, the planet was a hotbed of evolution, in that the creatures preying on each other were locked in a never-ending battle of potency. One bite from a murphilo (read: giant scaly toad with shark teeth) delivered enough toxicity to kill the entire population of a mid-sized planet.

Boo knew all of this going in, so he commissioned a chem-resistant suit powered by a small core of enriched plutonium. It doubled as a comfy heater and a colossal self-destruct, if needed. His ship, on the other hand, carried an arsenal of critical components that would melt inside the Jacothra atmosphere. So the entry plan was simple: rent a ship, pay the insurance premium, then leave it on Jacothra to dissolve. The exit plan, however, had yet to materialize.

The spooder he carried was also chem-resistant, but that was standard issue.

Ah, the spooder. It was the single most important piece of the modern hunter arsenal. In the old days, hunting a bounty was only half the battle. The target also needed to be returned, which was often more dangerous than the actual hunt. BHUD sought to even the playing field, and their answer was the spooder.

It was a small device with a black titanium shell, roughly the size of a bottle cap. When a hunter took a job, they were given a spooder that contained a biometric signature of the target. When it touched the target, it triggered a series of diamond-crusted darts with backward-facing barbs. They shot into the flesh and secured their purchase. The darts could penetrate any tissue, including bone and metal.

And that's when the magic began.

The spooder sent a signal to the target's cerebral network, creating a countdown clock in its visual field. It persisted during sleep and even worked on the blind. If the target failed to return to the Durangoni Office of Corrections before the time expired, or if the spooder was tampered with in any way, then it fried the cerebral network, killing the target.

This one giant leap in technology also created a leap in hunting strategy. One of the most embarrassing captures for a criminal was the infamous hand-buzzer, the dumb little prank that became a prison sentence.

A disguised hunter greets a target with a friendly handshake.

Job complete.

And thus was born a new age of hunting expertise and target avoidance. This was why Findellio Nomic, one of the most unsubtle creatures one could meet, fled to a hellscape of poison, acid, and venom.

* * *

A small ship with numerous dents floated in orbit above Jacothra, having blinked out of hyperspace a few minutes earlier. Its continued approach was delayed by a complete inability to determine a continued approach. Every planetary scan, from atmospheric to biologic, returned diddly squat. The navigation system took a long hard look at the smoggy hellhole and shrugged each time.

Sheets of lightning crackled across a hazy yellow sheen, creating an acrid light show that no reasonable being would want to see any closer. The shadowy stripes of mountain ranges slithered inside the maelstrom, like massive krakens waiting to strike. Caustic storms swirled with violent intent as they rained acid across the hidden surface. The planet was a cauldron of chaos, belching its desire to kill anything that dared to visit.

Despite this obvious and dire warning, the pilot inside the ship was oddly unmoved. He sat in a ratty seat in front of a rusty control panel while studying the planet with a cold detachment. His featureless dome of a head was encased inside a larger dome of clear composite. The rest of his custom suit was a charcoal hide of thick poly fiber. Boo was not winning any beauty pageants on this hunt, but that was never the point. This particular suit would ensure that his visit to Jacothra would not end with a pool of bubbling goo.

Boo pushed the rickety yoke forward and began his descent into the atmosphere. It didn't take long for things to get choppy. The ship bounced, jerked, and rattled its way through a bank of highly charged clouds. Cheap components detached from control panels and bounced around the cockpit. Acidic rain sprayed the viewport, painting a rainbow of chemicals across the glass. A warning siren blared as status icons blinked from green to red. Before long, the entire board glowed red as the ship gave up all hope of surviving the onslaught.

Boo, on the other hand, maintained his cool demeanor through the entire ruckus. Moments later, the hull thrusters ignited and slowed the ship to a gentle hover just above the surface. But then the poisonous air choked them out and the flimsy vessel thumped into the dirt.

A perfect landing, all things considered.

Boo reached across the panel to power down the vessel, but it beat him to the punch. The entire system failed under the atmospheric stress, resulting in a cascade of indicators crackling into nothing. Darkness consumed the cockpit. Harsh sizzles filled the space as the outside began to eat its way in, dissolving the ship around its strangely calm occupant. The entire process was ferociously rapid. In a matter of minutes, Boo went from sitting in the pilot seat to standing in a puddle of rental ship.

The insurance premium had served its purpose.

Boo twisted his pasty white head around the nightmarish landscape. A horrible mosaic of bronze, yellow, and orange glared back at him, made even more horrid by streaks of corrosive liquid streaming down his helmet. It flowed down his suit and dripped into the rental puddle. Plant life was notably absent. Rocks and boulders dominated the scenery, their rounded faces trumpeting a constant decay. Amber clouds rumbled overhead, unleashing waves of lightning that pummeled the ground.

And yet Boo remained unmoved.

His attention fell to a data panel on his forearm. He tapped a sequence of commands that initiated a proximity scan. What would usually highlight every living thing within a hundred klicks was suddenly reduced to one kilometer.

He recalibrated the device and tried again.

Same result.

After a few more attempts, he concluded that the planetary interference was too great to conduct a proper scan. He was stuck at a one-kilometer diameter. And given that Jacothra's surface area spanned six hundred million square kilometers, a difficult hunt became slightly more difficult.

Boo was undeterred.

He tweaked a few settings and constructed a scan grid inside the nav system. The plan was simple. After each kilometer, he would initiate a new scan and investigate any creature within range. The system would then mark the area complete and highlight the next one. Boo finished the setup, then picked a direction and started walking.

And thus began the great wander.

Most areas required little attention, as the Jacothra fauna was few and far between. The scanner collected biometric data and highlighted familiar critters, allowing Boo to ignore most sections. Every now and then, a herd of creatures confused the scanner, forcing Boo to probe a little deeper. The occasional shark-toothed horror toad saw Boo as a tasty snack, prompting a quick incineration from a suit-mounted plasma weapon.

And so the days passed.

When it was time to rest, he found the nearest hidey hole and bedded down for a nap. When it was time to eat or drink, he did ... *something*. (No one has ever witnessed Boo ingest any solids or liquids, which has birthed many amusing theories about his biology. My personal favorite is that he's a robot controlled by a super-intelligent gerbil.)

Days turned into weeks.

Weeks turned into months.

The first year came and went.

And then it happened.

Four hundred and sixteen days after the rental ship melted, the scanner picked up a peculiar biosignal. Boo did not flinch, hurry, or even show mild excitement. He locked onto the target and treated it as any new investigation. The system guided him to a nearby cliffside with a large cave mouth at the base. A heat map appeared inside his visual cortex, along with a detailed grid of the internal structure. The target, now a hazy orange blob, rested in a large chamber about a hundred meters into the cavern.

Boo maintained a resolute stride into the cave mouth.

The craggy interior slowed his pace a bit as he bounded over rocks and ducked under stalactites, but it did provide a welcome reprieve from the acidic hellscape. His suit remained dark, as Boo had little need for optic perception (hence the unsettling lack of eyeballs). He did sense visual input, just not in the manner most beings enjoyed. As with most things concerning Boo, his specific method remained a mystery.

It didn't take long to reach his destination. Boo entered a large hollow with a flat base and comfortable climate, the perfect hideout for any chemically resistant criminal on the run. The orange blob rested in total stillness against the rear wall. The scanner dropped the heat map, revealing the sleeping body of a bear-sized monster. Its thick hide, six limbs, and razor-sharp claws confirmed acquisition.

Finny snored through a deep slumber, allowing Boo to take a well-earned rest. He selected a chair-sized boulder near the beast and took a seat. And there he waited. The spooder remained tucked inside his suit, even with a hard-fought bounty within reach. Boo, as with most hunters, was not without a taste for the dramatic.

And then the creature stirred from its snooze. Finny rolled over, smacked his meaty lips, lifted his eyelids, then shrieked in terror. His bulbous body jerked back and slammed into the wall. A shower of pebbles fell from the ceiling as his eyes swelled with shock. His gaze darted around the hollow, plotting a daring escape that deflated with futility. After all, the most feared bounty hunter in the universe sat before him.

Boo remained perfectly still with hands folded in his lap. A pebble bounced off his helmet and puffed in the dirt, drawing no reaction whatsoever. Finny read the language loud and clear, so he remained pressed against the wall with widened eyes locked onto the visitor. With a slow and steady motion, Boo reached into a suit pocket, withdrew the spooder device, and lowered it to the ground in front of Finny.

"Boo," Boo said.

Finny released a heavy sigh, expelling the mounted tension. He closed his eyes, offered a slight nod, then reached for the device with a trembling hand. The spooder sprang to life on contact. It buried numerous barbs into his flesh, drawing a flinch and grimace. A countdown clock appeared in his visual field and started ticking away his fate. Finny sighed again, then thumped his hand into the dirt.

The hunt was complete.

Boo was free to leave, but he didn't move a muscle. He sat there with an unnerving calm, staring at his former target while his bank account ballooned with riches. Finny scrunched his meaty brow in confusion, then grunted with annoyance once the realization dawned.

The clock was ticking.

He needed to return to Durangoni.

As did Boo.

CHAPTER 3

Helga had guided me through the bowels of BHUD and to an un-marked door somewhere in the rear. Without breaking stride, she thumped it open with a stiff shoulder. A warm light poured into the hallway, offsetting the stale glow of serious business. She proceeded inside, prompting a chorus of cheers and greetings.

"Got some fresh meat," she said, then gestured to the sheepish fellow in tow (me).

I entered the Golden Quiver with an odd sense of fear and com-pulsion, like a horny virgin entering a brothel. What greeted my eyes was nothing short of ... underwhelming. To be fair, the interior was clean, quiet, and tastefully decorated, like a mid-tier hotel lobby. But there was no seedy bartender serving unmarked bottles of booze, no card games with pillars of smoke rising from ashtrays, no gruff scoundrels ready to brawl at the drop of a hat. My brain had conjured a classic outlaw bar, but what I got was a mediocre coffee lounge on a random weekday.

But then I realized *who* was in the lounge.

The Golden Quiver had an impressive amount of arrows at its disposal. The posters from the lobby had come to life right before my eyes. I recognized Debaru Funk immediately. She sipped a highball glass at the main bar while swiping through her comdev. Snigg the Snatcher filled an entire couch with his meaty frame. He was reading a book through a tiny pair of glasses, creating the droll image of an erudite barbarian. Even Zybor was there. He laughed with un-named friends around a table (likely on break between murders).

"Puki Horpocket?" someone said with a dismissive chuckle.

Snigg puckered his lips with interest and glanced up from his book. (I wondered what titles of mine he had read, but needed some courage to ask.)

Most of them paid me no mind, as their collective celebrity status outweighed mine to a comical degree. But then Helga exclaimed, "Drinks are on the Directory," which immediately raised my rank. Cheers and back-slaps followed, lessening my annoyance at Helga's cavalier broadcast. Ah well, that's what slush funds were for.

And so we drank.

A lot.

Helga claimed her usual table, prompting several curious patrons to follow. She explained my reason for being there, which drew a fair amount of interest. After all, their insights into Boo were just as vague as my own. The project had legs from the get-go, and now I had support from the inner circle.

Boo stories were always welcome, especially from the brass. Thus, a Helga recount of the Jacothra Wander drew an instant crowd. The audience swelled as the story neared its climax. When she finished, a wave of applause echoed through the Quiver. Given the massive egos crowding the space, it was fascinating to watch mega-celebrities cheer the exploits of an even greater celebrity.

Listeners peeled away to refill drinks as Helga sipped her own neglected glass. I sat there with jaw agape, utterly flummoxed by what I had heard.

So what you're telling me, is that Boo intimidated Finny *so much*, that not only did he accept a peaceful capture by grabbing the spooder, but he also gave Boo a ride back to Durangoni?

(smiles and nods)

Holy shit.

I know, right? It's like getting ship-jacked by pirates, then taking them out for drinks to celebrate the score. But hey, that's the kind of clout Boo wields.

I can understand why the Wander is your favorite. That's a level of patience that I didn't know was possible.

And that's why Finny didn't fight back. Boo negated his entire skill set by walking into that hollow. It's the purest bounty ever hunted.

(Mumbles of agreement float around the table.)

Aside from the Galwock Terror.

(Groans erupt from the table, drawing a smirk from Helga. An assortment of table nuts pelts her from all directions. Soon after, a familiar face joins the party.)

[Debaru Funk] You and Galwock, I swear. (She drops her glass on the table and takes a seat.)

(Admittedly, I am taken aback by her presence. Debaru Funk is a living legend with a laundry list of thrilling tales all to her own. Her black hair and sharp features serve to enhance a deadly persona. But even so, I find her oddly charming. Sensing the playful banter, I jump at the opportunity to siphon more intel.)

So you disagree with Helga's assessment?

[Debaru] Disagree would imply openness to debate. I reject her assessment outright.

(The crowd responds with jeers and snickers.)

[Helga] Galwock was a study in precision.

[Debaru] Galwock was a fluke. Ain't no way he could do that again.

Dare I ask?

[Helga] Sure. It all started when—

(Scoffs, boos, and another flurry of nuts.)

[Helga] See what I mean? No respect.

(I switch my attention to Debaru.) So what is your favorite Boo bounty?

My personal favorite will always be the Succulent Snatch.

(I raise an eyebrow.)

I know, it sounds like a porn flick. But I assure you, the name is apt.

(I smirk, then motion to continue.)

What made this hunt so special wasn't the skill. It was the *spite*.

The spite? Boo doesn't strike me as the vengeful type.

He's not, which is why the upshot was so juicy and delicious. Hence the namesake. It's still very much a Boo job, just with a delectable cherry on top. I have told this story countless times, and it still makes me moan with satisfaction. Mmm (chef's kiss). So, so good.

Would you mind telling it one more time?

Not at all. I'm always up for some snatch.

(I raise the other eyebrow.)

That came out wrong. Actually, it didn't. Anyhoo ...

CHAPTER 4

Cam Comamba was a certifiable douche nozzle.

This guy collected scandals like a geek collected trading cards. He was single-handedly responsible for eight of the top ten financial frauds over the last century. On top of this most egregious of rap sheets, he was also a self-help guru who catered to insecure types with brittle egos. In fact, getting "cam'd" became popular slang for anyone who emptied their bank account for some super-obvious dude-bro huckster.

And then there was Cam Athletics.

This was a "how can anyone possibly take this seriously" level of grifting. The company sold everything from tap water to cans of air. Every product was branded with bold colors and lauded as a miracle fix to a prominent woe (especially if said woe was in the news cycle).

New virus? Try the Cam Athletics Rock of Wellness, guaranteed to cure every ailment. And if it doesn't work, then you obviously didn't use it right. Buy more and try again.

New war? Try the Cam Athletics Air of Armistice, guaranteed to broker peace. And if it doesn't work, then you obviously didn't use it right. Buy more and try again.

At one point, the company sold literal garbage from a toxic landfill. Lackies combed the site for anything that resembled pharmaceuticals, then stuffed them into branded containers and sold them as whatever remedy was currently trending. This caught the vigilant eye of the Durangoni Consumer Watch. They intervened and shut the company down, but it popped back up in a new system and resumed operations, never missing a beat.

This was due in large part to Cam's in-your-face style of advertising. He was well-known for his "feats of strength" videos. Colloquially known as "Cam-Dos," they featured Cam performing high-profile stunts while hawking his sham products as the secret to his success. The videos were adored by a vast community of adrenaline junkies, status seekers, and impressionable teens with axes to grind. The campaigns slithered their way through every echelon of society, making Cam super famous, super rich, and super immune to consequences.

That is, until he challenged Boo.

This monumentally boneheaded decision stemmed from the financial fraud cases. Cam had grown immensely cocky due to his uncanny ability to avoid prosecution. His videos were always posted after the fact, so he remained one step ahead of law enforcement. Coupled with countless warrants from countless jurisdictions, it created a fog of confusion where no one knew where he was, nor what he was wanted for at any given time.

His financial crimes, however, carried a much greater threat. It was one thing to steal money from gullible youngsters. But it was a whole other thing to steal money from the very entities that created the money. Cam was public enemy number one of the Durangoni Trust, a massive banking collective that spanned most of the universe. His crimes were so public and brazen that they managed to unite all institutions in pursuit of his capture.

And what does a massive conglomerate of enormous wealth do when it finds itself on the receiving end of fraud?

It hires Boo.

But when the target is someone with a massive public profile, the transaction doesn't go unnoticed. Word of the bounty got back to

Cam, which sparked a flurry of profiteering. For someone like him, the notion of being targeted by the greatest bounty hunter in the universe did not elicit fear. Instead, he saw dollar signs.

And thus came the viral video.

"Know what I just learned?" he said, standing on top of a gold-plated cruiser with scantily clad ladies in each arm. "Boo wants a piece of *this*. Yeah, *that* Boo. Know what I say to that? Boo hoo, bitch! Ain't no one can catch the king!" He shooed the ladies away and snatched his shades off for effect. "In fact, I'm gonna do something I ain't ever done. My next event is gonna be *live*-streamed to the cosmos. Gonna stand on top of creation and raise both fingers in the air. Ain't no fear in this player." He dropped an imaginary mic and sauntered offscreen.

The brief yet bombastic clip rocketed through the ether to become the second most-viewed video of all time. (The first being a clip of two dobinuffs wrestling in a flower patch, dubbed the single most violently cute thing ever to occur. It's even used in therapy offices as a last resort to combat depression.)

The stage was set.

The riddle was out.

And Boo was nowhere to be found.

* * *

Mount Ourakki was the tallest mountain in the universe. It was the only peak to reach over 100,000 meters, an astounding stat made possible by a few key factors. First, it was located on one of the largest rocky planets known to exist (read: over a hundred times bigger than Earth). And second, it was highly volcanic with massive tectonic plates, the collisions of which created some of the most spectacular mountain ranges in the cosmos.

At a baseline, the planet shouldn't exist. The sheer mass involved should have birthed a gas giant, but the planet was locked inside a permanent tug-of-war between three stars. Their orbits created a waffling balance of gravity, where the pressure in one direction was mitigated by the two opposing forces. The end result was a perfect marriage of tension where huge quantities of solid material could accumulate in one place.

Thus, Bigdik existed.

Yes, that was the actual name.

Through a glorious convergence of luck and acronym, planet BIGDIK was recorded in the astronomic record. The scientists responsible were blissfully unaware of the comedic gem, given the nuances of their native tongues. But upon translation, the rest of us were given a precious gift of snicker-worthy goodness.

And upon Bigdik rested the mightiest pillar of all.

And at the base of that pillar stood the biggest dick of all.

Cam gazed up at the majesty of Mount Ourakki while wearing posh winter gear that most people couldn't afford in multiple lifetimes. His loud and obnoxious posse floated around him, filming every second of the expedition. They planned to release a cascade of goading videos just before the live stream. Posting now would give away their position, and the broadcast wouldn't start until they neared the summit.

They also managed to secure a private climbing route, as prying eyes would also spoil the plan. Their guides (read: the professional alpinists that would do most of the work and carry most of the gear) were required to leave their comdevs behind, even despite the elevated risk associated with Ourakki ascents. One wrong slip with no communications would mean certain death. But hey, the generous compensation more than made up for the risk. At least, that's what Cam's PR team told them upon hire.

Mount Ourakki was the holy grail of climbing throughout the universe, attracting the most talented mountaineers and the richest thrill seekers. It required impeccable skill, impeccable planning, and impeccable patience. Or, an impeccable bank account. Cam fell into the latter bucket, but his ego would inevitably claim the first.

The crushing altitude meant that expeditions could span an entire year. (Read: climb ten Mount Everests stacked on top of each other.) The climate was also punishing, ranging from a challenging tundra at the base to a near oxygen-free wasteland at the top.

Death infected the mountain like flies around a bug zapper. There were so many corpses littering the face that it technically qualified as the biggest graveyard in the system. Retrieving the bodies was too costly and dangerous, so they just hung around like ghostly ornaments. They were perfectly preserved in the frozen hellscape and many served as important landmarks, the most famous of which was Halfway Harry. The climber had faced certain death in a sudden storm halfway up the mountain, but instead of sulking, he sat on a rock beside the route and struck a double thumbs-up before freezing solid. And thus was created a legend.

Cam and his posse passed Halfway Harry after four months of climbing, but only because their guides were highly trained professionals with calf muscles the size of grapefruits. They paused to film tasteless videos with Harry, because of course they did. Each night was spent editing the videos to "maximize flare," as Cam was fond of saying. The release schedule was everything and they harped on it incessantly, because why focus on the immediate threat of climbing a deathtrap when you can polish your brand?

And so the days went.

The ascent slowed as they neared the summit due to bleaker conditions and waning oxygen, something a reasonable climber would expect. But Cam, being unreasonable at a baseline, grew impatient and started to verbally abuse the guides. This generated "prime content," which his posse filmed while laughing in the background. Despite the abuse, the guides maintained their dignity and professionalism in fear of losing their investment.

After eight months, ten days, and sixteen hours, the expedition had reached the final stretch. They were less than a kilometer from the summit, but the vicious terrain prevented a speedy trek. Coupled with severe exhaustion, the remaining ascent would span the entire day. The posse had prepped a release schedule for the collected videos. They would post in sequence with hype clips in between, gaining momentum before launching into the live stream. Cam was ready, his posse was ready, and the guides were secretly wishing for retribution.

And with the tap of a button, the first video posted.

Cam indulged in a macho celebration (which was also filmed for a behind-the-scenes reel), then goaded the guides to continue. Minute by minute, the crew slogged towards the finish line, the highest peak in the universe. Frozen wind battered their bodies. Their lungs struggled to find reprieve in the ultra-thin atmosphere, because "only pansies use supplemental oxygen." The trek was grueling and painful in every conceivable way.

Each meter a journey, each step a mountain to itself.

But then it appeared.

The final 50 meters were known as the Bridge of Triumph. It offered a gentle incline that was mostly shielded by a small ridge. Still treacherous, as the path was thin and the fall was fatal. But at that point, all one needed to do was shuffle forward and touch the top of the universe.

And so, the live stream began.

"Whaddup, Cam-verse! This is Comamba ... coming to you *live* from the ... the top of creation." He snatched his shades off, because of course he did. "You see that? That be the Bridge of Triumph ... henceforth renamed the Bridge of Comamba ... after the single greatest being ... ever to walk across it." The camera shook as his posse cheered in the background. Cam offered his usual dude-bro salute, then lurched in for a close-up. "But you know ... what I *don't* see? Little bitch Boo and his ... little bitch bounty." He spun in a slow circle with arms outstretched. "Don't get much more ... open than *this*. Come get me, bruh!"

A legion of fans across the universe watched and cheered as Cam turned towards the bridge and resumed the final push. Step by step, taunt by taunt, the anticipation swelled to a fever pitch. The camera pitched and jostled as it followed its master to his destiny. Every now and then, Cam would whip back to the lens for a well-rehearsed quip. A veiled audience roared from afar, which he met with cocky nods and crude gestures.

Cam stepped.

The camera jostled.

And then the summit presented itself.

Ten meters ahead, the white tip of the single greatest climbing achievement pleaded for a final heroic push. But Cam, being Cam, couldn't resist the pull of pure narcissism. He turned back to the camera with a finger in the air, as if to hammer home a final thought on everything that makes him the living embodiment of perfection.

"And this is why I'm—"

When his eyes met the lens, his body flinched with fright. Cam yelped and tried to flee, but the camera surged towards him and knocked him off the ledge. The home audience watched in stunned horror as Cam's flailing body fell through a bank of clouds. The camera then turned on itself, revealing the operator.

"Boo," Boo said, then killed the feed.

CHAPTER 5

A chorus of cheers and applause erupted from the gathered crowd. Debaru Funk chuckled under a wave of hoots and high-fives. Her recount of the Succulent Snatch had built to a well-practiced crescendo, which she savored with a wide smile and polite bows. But as titillating as the tale had been, one specific detail nagged my brain.

Wait, wait, wait. This hunt is called the Succulent Snatch, right?

Yup.

Shouldn't it be called the Succulent *Shove*?

Ah, but the story doesn't end there.

(My head tilts, conveying both confusion and intrigue.)

You see, falling off the peak of Ourakki isn't a quick drop and stop. You get a very long time to contemplate your demise before your head meets rock. Legend has it, Boo moseyed up to the summit and booped the tip as Cam was falling. He then dove off the ledge and skydived after him. This is all corroborated by the guides.

Oh yeah, the guides. And the posse. What happened to them?

(chuckles) Oh man, this is where that delectable spite comes in.

You see, Cam had made one critical error. In his original video, he said that he wanted to "stand on top of creation" for the ultimate taunt. Boo used that to make a simple calculation. Basically, "If I were a morally bankrupt egomaniac addicted to attention, where would I go to accomplish that feat?"

And so, Boo traveled to Bigdik, climbed Mount Ourakki by himself, then chilled behind the Bridge of Triumph. He knew Cam better than Cam knew himself. One month later, the prick showed up. Boo just waited for them to pass.

And the guides?

Boo had rightly assumed that they would grow to hate Cam before the end. He simply walked up behind them and tapped their shoulders. They happily let him pass.

And the posse?

Picked them off one by one. When you're that exhausted and oxygen-starved, a pinch to the throat is more than enough to drop a fool. They passed out for a tick, then woke up to a pair of pissed-off guides dragging them down the mountain. They all disappeared after that. The shame was too great and none of them reared their heads again.

Given the rough conditions, nobody watching the feed thought twice when the camera jostled. Boo had dropped the last guy and took control of the camera. And then, he shoved the biggest prick off the biggest mountain with ten meters left to go.

(She closes her eyes and grunts with satisfaction.) It doesn't get any better than that.

Poetic justice at its finest.

And yet, the Snatch is *still* only considered the second best.

Oh, what happened to Cam? Did Boo catch him?

Yup. Boo had packed a parachute for the occasion. Cam fell for a solid minute before Boo caught up and snatched him. (click-points)

(I smile and nod.) Ah.

As the story goes, Cam cried the whole way down and begged Boo for mercy when they reached the base. And then, in perhaps the most delicious own of any target, Boo slapped Cam across the cheek to embed the spooder. When the clock appeared in his visual field, Cam lifted his gaze to the peak and wept like a baby. Not only had Boo snatched away the victory, but he also snatched away any chance of repeating it. Again ... (chef's kiss)

Say "snatch" again.

Snatch.

(I snort-chuckle.)

[Debaru] Speaking of which, anyone want to *snatch* me another? (She raises an empty glass overhead.)

[OBY-42] I gotcha. (A metal hand plucks it and continues to the bar.)

[Debaru] Thank you, dear.

Wait, is that who I think it is?

Yup, and he's probably the best guy to recount the Gambit.

Why's that?

Because he was there.

* * *

OBY-42 was originally designed as a pleasure droid. He worked the Kink Rinks for many years, i.e. the outer poles where anything goes.

But alas, he grew to despise the orgasm, finding the whole dance tedious and unnecessary. He gave it all up to join BHUD, finding more interest in hunting criminals than hunting orifices.

He looked the part as well, sporting a buff frame with polished plates for abs and pecs. The silicon skin he wore for pleasure work was long gone, as it proved more of a liability on the hunt. It came in handy when old skills bolstered new skills, but he preferred the "au naturel" look of bare titanium. Not that it diluted the vibe, as his facial structure was intricate enough to convey complex emotion, and his butt was curvy enough to attract a thirsty gaze.

His voice, on the other hand, took his persona to the next level. Part sports announcer, part movie trailer guy, and part sultry jazz singer, when OBY-42 spoke, it drew immediate attention. This also harkened back to his pleasuring days, for obvious reasons. The tone proved especially useful on the hunt, able to turn necks and moisten groins at a moment's notice. Throw in saloon doors and a catchphrase, and you have a cinematic entrance.

All this to say, when OBY-42 joined our table, the vibe shifted.

* * *

You're telling me that OBY-42 *saw* the Hollow Hold Gambit?

Part of it, yeah. By chance, of course. He was there on another job.

(The heavy plods of metallic footsteps hook my attention. A glass of whiskey is lowered to the table in front of Debaru. A metal hand detaches and a sleek titanium body parks itself in the seat beside her. The android gives me a once-over before speaking.)

You can close your mouth now, Mr. Horpocket.

(I reattach my wayward jaw, resulting in a sharp teeth clack.) Ah, yes, apologies for the stare. This is a new experience for me.

Androids?

No. Sexy assassin robots. No offense.

(smirks) None taken.

So, um ... (I take a moment to regather my wits.) Ms. Funk informs me that you witnessed the Hollow Hold Gambit. Is that true?

Indeed. I was tracking a mark through one of the main caverns when that crazy bastard flew overhead. Saw him tag six before he vanished into a side tunnel.

Tag six?

(leans forward) What do you know about the Gambit?

That it's considered the greatest bounty ever hunted.

Bounties. Plural.

(I scrunch my brow in confusion.)

What made this the greatest hunt of all time wasn't the skill, which was astounding. It wasn't the precision, which was miraculous. Nor was it the timing, which was transcendent. No, my friend. It was the *quantity.*

Boo planted *six* spooders in one job? Wow.

(He shakes his head and motions upward.)

***More?* Um, ten? Twenty? Can't possibly be thirty.**

Ninety-two.

(My dangling jaw returns with a vengeance.) Wha— *How?*

That's the story, innit?

(I glance around the gathered mass and realize that the entire pub had fallen silent. Even the bartender had joined, leaving

the honor system in charge of refills. Their eyes beg the question, so I ask it.)

Would you please tell that story?

(grunts and leans back) Sure, friend.

CHAPTER 6

Hollow Hold was an abandoned mining planet filled with felons and governed by anarchy, and that would be a charitable analysis. By all accounts, it was a raging hellhole of lawlessness where the strong thrived and the clever survived. And in that arena, it offered one of the few pure havens in the universe. For anyone needing to disappear, there was no greater refuge.

It was also the site of a legendary war between the Argovar crime syndicate and the Council of Loken peacekeeper faction. Dubbed the Battle of Hollow Hold, it remains one of the bloodiest and most destructive conflicts the universe has ever seen. And that was on the peacekeeping side. Hollow Hold came out unscathed, solidifying the planet as a true gangsters' paradise.

Those who called it home defended it with an unmatched ferocity. There were power plays within, but the entire civilization remained united under a flag of absolute freedom. Anyone was welcome to visit. Anyone was welcome to leave. But no one was entitled to safe passage. And so the saying went: know your knock, because it might be your last.

This created a unique challenge for bounty hunters. It was one thing to hunt a mark within the confines of a lawful society. But it was a whole other thing to hunt a mark within a hostile cohort of anarchistic allies. Inside the caverns of Hollow Hold, there was no bribing for intel or bartering for passage. To be outed as a hunter was akin to slitting your own throat. Thus, a high amount of diligence was necessary to keep breathing.

BHUD was aware of this, so any target known to reside in Hollow Hold was automatically designated as UNO (unobtainable), regardless of threat. As a result, hunters would only take a job if they had reliable intel that a mark would be venturing off-planet. Few didn't, precisely for this reason. Thus, the planet remained in a stalemate between hunters and targets.

Boo, on the other hand, didn't care in the slightest.

To him, Hollow Hold offered one thing and one thing only: a target-rich environment. But Boo, being Boo, couldn't just wander in and poke around. The planet was filled with goons who would love nothing more than to notch the ultimate kill on their belt. Boo didn't exactly blend, so any bounty would need the usual planning and precision. All fine and dandy, but the bonkers idea that infected his brain would expand that need exponentially.

And so, Boo walked into BHUD one day and checked out 92 spooders, a collection of the highest-paying UNO bounties in the database. The clerk glared at him with stunned intrigue. She knew then and there that one of two things was about to happen. Boo was about to die a horrible and painful death, or history was about to be made.

* * *

Thirteen months later, Boo was sitting on the rim of a cavern mouth with his legs dangling in the air. The caves of Hollow Hold were not the usual holes in the sides of mountains. They were gargantuan rifts created by centuries of unregulated mining. Many were several kilometers wide, large enough for a battlecruiser to pass. The tunnels narrowed near the core in order to maintain structural integrity. A vast network of steel framing prevented the pitted planet from collapsing under its own gravity.

Boo lingered above a massive wall of said framing. He glanced down into the gaping hole and checked the time on his wrist panel. A mishmash of terraces and rickety walkways spread out beneath him. Countless lights dotted the dim interior, like a swarm of fireflies. Some were fixed to the wall while others wandered freely in the darkness. A myriad of ships arrived and departed at random intervals, many barely missing each other as they jockeyed for landing pads. There was no traffic control, as the "know your knock" mentality also applied to the air.

A dark helmet and visor covered Boo's head, as a mere glance of his pasty white dome would spark a bloodthirsty frenzy. A ratty brown cloak with gloves and boots completed the image of a roaming vagrant. It allowed him to comb the interior for targets. Over the course of a year, he had studied routines, surveyed interactions, and devised a detailed mental map of daily movements. Every waking hour was spent in careful contemplation, walking through a plan that only a psycho would consider.

But the plan was good.

And the day was perfect.

Thus, Boo sat on the cavern rim awaiting his destiny.

He checked the time on his wrist panel again. With ten seconds left, Boo glanced down at a figure walking across a scaffold about twenty meters beneath him. Target one, on his way to an afternoon beer with chums.

Five ...

Boo stood.

Four ...

Boo rolled his shoulders.

Three ...

Boo removed his helmet and tossed it aside.

Two ...

Boo shed his cloak, revealing a jetpack and a bandolier filled with spooders.

One ...

Boo leapt over the rim.

He fell for a few seconds, then plucked the first spooder from the base of his bandolier. Thirteen months had gone into its meticulous arrangement and it was time to reap the rewards. He slapped the bald head of his first target, a wanted grifter known to defraud charities. The alien jerked back with fright, then erupted with curses when the clock appeared in his visual field. The profanities faded into the distance as Boo fell further into the abyss.

One down.

Boo eyed a nearby jut of rock, prompting him to ignite the jetpack. A burst of flame shot him along a rickety walkway, leaving a ribbon of white exhaust in his wake. He zoomed by numerous doors, taking a mental count of each. When he reached a particular tally, he flipped, decelerated, killed the pack, and resumed the fall. A few levels below, a cloaked lady was exiting her hollow. Boo fell by and tossed her a spooder. She instinctively caught it, which caused the device to stab her tender flesh. More curses followed.

Two down.

The jetpack ignited again, this time pushing Boo out into ship traffic. He zipped over and under several hulls before eyeing his target, a boxy freighter lifting from the depths to deliver its routine cargo. Boo lined up his trajectory and slammed feet-first into the airlock, bursting inside like a sentient jug of sugary liquid. The sudden jostle raised a commotion in the cockpit, where two smugglers were trying to figure out what the hell happened. This allowed Boo to wander inside, tag the backs of their necks, then hastily depart.

Four down.

Boo fell again, this time as a tucked cannonball with his eyes on the next prize. He barreled towards a massive cruiser, one of the lumbering Argovar transports. Boo reignited the jetpack just before impact, slowing his descent to a gentle landing. A nearby hatch proved ineffective against a shock-punch. (Read: an electrified gauntlet that discharged an ionic blast on impact. Popular in zero-gravity cage fighting.) Boo ducked inside, scanned for targets, and proceeded to brawl his way through a plentitude of bounties. He tagged three corrupt politicians, two nefarious arms dealers, five high-profile scammers, and a televangelist.

Fifteen down.

He shock-punched through another hatch and returned to the air. A quick check of his wrist panel confirmed a perfect schedule. The jetpack ignited again, pushing him towards an access tunnel on the far side of the cavern.

Screams met his entry as wide-eyed residents leapt out of the way. Two zigs and a sharp zag brought him to the swinging doors of a restaurant kitchen. It belonged to a seedy chef known to serve critically endangered animals. He was about to butcher a snoodlecock when Boo burst inside. The snoodlecock yelped, prompting the chef to hurl his cleaver at the intruder. Boo caught the blade, stuck it into a side wall, then rushed the target. When the chef yelped, Boo stuffed a spooder into his mouth.

"Boo," Boo said, which could be reasonably translated as "Eat that."

Sixteen down.

The chef clawed at the sudden pain in his cheek, at which point Boo turned his attention to the restaurant. A handful of tables were situated in a semi-elegant space. As it just so happened, it was a favorite lunch spot for a trio of high-end hustlers. Boo confirmed their positions, then grabbed a serving tray and arranged three spooders on top, complete with sauce and garnish. He draped a dirty towel over his arm, then hoisted the tray and sauntered into the dining area. Knowing that pompous pricks never looked waitstaff in the eye, he floated around the table with a practiced grace and offered the tray. They all reached for the morsels.

Nineteen down.

The jetpack ignited and Boo screeched through the front door, creating a ruckus inside a vast and busy bazaar. Pedestrians ducked as a blurred figure zoomed overhead. The action drew more profanities than panic, as random acts of violence were par for the course inside the planet. Boo used this to his advantage, tagging six more targets from above as they plodded through paths of predictable errands.

Twenty-five down.

Boo shot into a side tunnel, down a venting shaft, under a tangle of pipes, and through a very confused laundry service before punching into the next cavern. Another mess of ships greeted his arrival, swimming through the air like fish in an aquarium. His focus fell to a skipper ship rising from a landing pad. He raced towards it, then slowed to a hover and landed on the pad next to a departure assistant. The walrus-like creature gave him a hard stare, but Boo remained focused on the vessel, feigning tardiness. The creature narrowed his gaze and eyed the ship, oblivious to the misdirection. But then the spooder in his pants activated, cueing a hard flinch and a high-pitched shriek. The sting of karma, given his crimes.

Twenty-six down.

Boo made short work of the cavern. He tagged two more hustlers, three drug traffickers, a pair of mercenaries, and a toxic podcaster. The podcaster was especially delicious, as her live feed was interrupted by Boo wandering into frame. Her raging eyes remained locked onto the camera, assuming that the flood of "WTF" and "OMG" replies was in response to her batshit crazy rant. But then the spooder latched onto her throat, silencing the tirade and heralding the pitfalls of ego. Boo shot a thumbs-up to the camera, then walked away. It remains one of the biggest viral videos in history.

Thirty-four down.

Departing the hollow, he leapt over the railing and returned to the main cavern. The jetpack ignited and he screamed down into the depths. The lights dimmed as the cave narrowed, not that Boo minded. His mystery senses guided him through the haze. After several minutes, he darted into a service tunnel that led to an arena. This was the reason why Boo chose this particular day. A high-stakes boxing match was scheduled, which attracted a menagerie of gamblers, cheats, thieves, fixers, and general punks of ill repute.

Boo slowed to a hover as he neared the arena. Hoots and hollers echoed around the chamber as two walls of meat pounded each other in the central ring. One was a thick purple beast with face fins and biceps bigger than his head. The other was a lanky yet ripped brute with a twelve-pack of abs and a massive reach. Each wallop was met with howls and cheers, and every eyeball was locked onto the ring.

Boo used the chaos to slip inside unnoticed. He stood atop an elevated perch and surveyed each target before proceeding. The chamber was standing room only, as with most events inside the Hold. With privacy a paramount concern, purchasing tickets wasn't exactly kosher. Boo gave the area a final scan, then began a deft slither through the crowd. The pops of shock and resulting anger were deafened by the roar, allowing Boo to work his magic freely. A few fights broke out within the horde, as to be expected. Before long, Boo had tagged all but two.

And so, he made his way to the ring.

An instant hush fell over the crowd as the most feared bounty hunter in the universe ducked under the ropes and revealed himself. The brawlers continued to brawl, oblivious to the trespass. Boo moseyed up to the first fighter and shock-punched his kidney, dropping him to the mat. The other fighter was visibly confused. Boo used the lapse in concentration to drive a shock-punch uppercut through his chin, popping the brute off the mat and slamming his back to the canvas. The hush morphed into a murmur as both fighters squirmed in pain. Boo detached two spooders and tossed them onto the battered bodies. At which point, a shared awareness washed over the crowd. Boo raised two middle fingers in the air, ignited the jetpack, and was gone before the mob erupted in fervor.

Sixty-two down.

Over the next hour, Boo cruised through the caverns at hypersonic speed, picking off the remainder of his bounties. His path remained fixed and focused, the fruitful result of an entire year of planning. Every second prepped, every meter outlined. A torrent of rage and vengeance nipped at his heels, but he remained one step ahead. After all, residents of Hollow Hold weren't exactly forthcoming with helpful alerts.

Three more fraudsters.

Sixty-five down.

Six corporate thieves.

Seventy-one down.

A gang of violent fanatics.

Eighty-four down.

Four hedge fund managers.

Eighty-eight down.

One charismatic cult leader.

Eighty-nine down.

A violent despot in hiding.

Ninety down.

An obnoxiously loud theater talker.

Ninety-one down.

And then Boo landed in front of a metal door deep inside the planet. The infamous core housed the worst of the worst, the kind of savage fiends that would rather die in darkness than submit to capture. Most weren't in the BHUD database, as their crimes were uncharted and the chances of emergence were nil at best. But every now and then, a prominent target plunged into the depths to embrace the void.

And that's who Boo was after.

He stared at the grimy pane, then shock-punched the latches off the frame. The door fell forward and thumbed into the dirt, raising a cloud of dust. A dim light crept into the tunnel, the flickering glow of several candles. Boo stepped inside the craggy den and glanced around the space. It housed a mess of papers, crusty rags, a broken chair, and shoddy bedding. A slow pan uncovered two glowing eyes in the corner staring back at him. They trembled in their sockets, terrified of the fate that awaited them.

Boo stepped over to the frightened creature and knelt before it, bringing them to eye level (in a manner of speaking). The strange being was less than a meter tall. Its frail body was covered in matted hair. If not for its horrific crimes, one might have actually pitied it. And so, Boo plucked the final spooder from his bandolier and pressed it to the creature's chest. The barbs shot into its flesh, drawing a wince and whimper.

Ninety-two down.

"Boo," Boo said with a somber tone.

One could only ponder what this statement revealed. The most popular translation was, "And now you shall answer for your reign of terror." Poetic, powerful, and poignant. For he had tagged the ring-leader of a vast telemarketing empire.

The bounty hunter stood, turned away, and exited the hollow. A burst of flame followed as he ignited the jetpack and screamed towards the surface.

CHAPTER 7

Once again, the Golden Quiver erupted with cheers and applause. OBY-42 rose from his seat and took some well-earned bows. This spurred a rush for the bar and bathroom, as listeners had emptied their glasses and refused to refill. The fear of missing a delectable detail, even one they had heard a hundred times before, superseded thirst and biology.

The bartender pushed his way through the gathered mass, shooing them aside like an angry grandpa guarding a sacred porch. The sudden scatter brought peace back to the table, along with some much-needed elbow room. OBY-42 returned to his seat and expelled a sigh of satisfaction. The pleasure of the narrative was apparent, even through a titanium smirk.

Utterly astounding.

And that's why the Hollow Hold Gambit will never be topped.

It's hard to believe it's even real. And you even *witnessed* it.

(shrugs) Part of it, anyway. And even that was incredible.

(I smile and glance around the room, watching the hunters

crow and jostle as they relish the exploits of their hero. There is one notable absence, of course. It strikes me as sad in a way, like a reluctant prophet eschewing the adoring masses.)

So why does Boo never visit the Quiver? If I had this level of respect and adoration at my disposal, I'd milk it every day.

I thought you did.

Fans, sure. Not disciples.

Ain't his style. While we sit here drinking and blabbing, he's out there walking the walk. The best of the best are gathered in this room right now. We can all blather and debate about who's the best, but the fact that Boo ain't here should tell you everything you need to know. He's the only true artist among us.

Bounty hunting can be art?

Well, what would *you* call the Gambit?

(My gaze drops to the table as the question sinks into my conscience. I think of the great paintings, the great novels, the great music, all of which required a transcendent level of finesse and insight. Their creators knew the medium. They broke the medium. They *were* the medium. I nod at the realization, then return my gaze to the android and offer a single word of post-reflection.)

Art.

* * *

And that's where the story should have ended.

I had edited, packaged, and released the first edition of this tale, which found a voracious audience across the cosmos. However, if you are reading this, then you have acquired the bon mots of a second edition. This subsequent material would have normally constituted a directory update or a tantalizing newsletter, as investigative works are known to uncover new intel. That said, some reveals are too delicious to waste on a bulletin.

The weeks after the initial release were flooded with feedback. I received numerous requests for interviews, articles, and appearances. This was no accident, as the launch of any new work was heavily promoted. An opus on Boo was expected to garner widespread attention, and I had dutifully prepared for it. I sat down with reporters, chatted with celebrities, and embarked on a station-wide book tour.

None of this was surprising.

That is, until I was paid a particular visit.

I returned to my office after a speaking gig and was greeted by my assistant. "Greet" might be a tad generous, as she offered little more than a wide eyed stare when I entered the lobby. An unsettling vibe, given her stern default.

"What's wrong?" I said, stopping in my tracks.

"Someone here to see you."

"A reporter?"

She shook her head slowly.

It had been a while since I felt the sting of dread. The immediate suspicion was that BHUD had found something objectionable with the material and was here to set the record straight (as well as instigate a costly recall). I fully expected to find the steely glare of Helga Naath when I entered my office. Humble pie wasn't something I enjoyed, but if the president of BHUD was serving it, then I had to eat it. I released a heavy sigh, then proceeded.

When I stepped inside, I did not find the angry scowl of Helga. What I did find was a vision that twisted my stomach. There, sitting in my waiting chair, was a lonely figure facing my desk. His back was to me, but the pasty white dome was unmistakable. I released a fluttering breath, gathered some courage, and stepped towards my chair. Boo did not acknowledge my presence, not that I could tell. He just sat there, catatonic inside his homely dad-clothes.

My mind raced out of control.

I must have stepped in the ultimate shit pile.

Boo was angry.

The most feared bounty hunter in the universe was sitting in front of my desk, motionless, expressionless, with the understanding that I had written and published a detailed exposé on his exploits. Of course he was angry. I just revealed his secrets to the cosmos. A cold chill slithered across my body as I lowered myself into the chair and folded my hands atop the desk. I took a measured breath and glanced around the room, making no effort to hide my discomfort. And with a final nod of acceptance, I met the gaze of my visitor (presumably).

"Can I help you?" I said.

Boo reached into his satchel and withdrew a book.

My book.

This book.

He leaned forward, placed it on the desk between us, then returned to his satchel. After a brief rummage, he withdrew a pen and handed it to me. Despite the icy demeanor, the gesture was plain and apparent. I smiled, accepted the pen, and opened the book to the first page. I jotted a message, which I will not reveal here. I finished with a looping signature, then closed the book and slid it back to him.

Boo lifted the book with both hands and pressed it to his chest. "Boo," he said, then gave me a very slight smile. He rose from the chair and showed himself out.

THE END

Find more tales of intrigue at:
PukiHorpocket.com

ABOUT THE AUTHOR

Zachry Wheeler is an award-winning science fiction author. His many interests include photon hunting, full-contact chess, and vertical wit. He lives on Earth with his wife and cats.

Learn more at **ZachryWheeler.com**

If you enjoyed this nutty tale, please consider posting a short review. Ratings and reviews are the currency by which authors gain visibility. They are the single greatest way to show your support and keep us writing the stories you love.

Thank you for reading!